The Candle in the Window

Written by **Grace Johnson**
Illustrated by **Mark Elliott**

Fleming H. Revell
A Division of Baker Book House Co
Grand Rapids, Michigan 49516

Published by Fleming H. Revell
a division of Baker Book House Company
P.O. Box 6287, Grand Rapids, MI 49516-6287

Based on "The Cobbler" by Grace Johnson, published in *Christmas by the Hearth,* Tyndale House Publishers, © 1996.

Art direction by Brian Brunsting and Cheryl Van Andel.

Printed in Singapore

Library of Congress Cataloging-in-Publication Data is on file at the Library of Congress, Washington, D.C.

ISBN 0-8007-1815-1

Scripture references are taken from the King James Version of the Bible.

*Once upon a time
in a little German village . . .*

. . . there lived a cobbler named Gunther. In the windows of his little shop, shoes and boots waited for their owners to claim them. Inside it smelled of shoe wax and the leather that was strewn on and around the cobbler's bench. And on any given day, except Sundays, Gunther would be hard at work—cutting, pounding, and stitching. In all the countryside there was not a finer cobbler.

Today was December 24. Snow had begun to fall, and the wind blew hard. Gunther was bent over his bench when in swept a stately gentleman whom Gunther immediately recognized. "Lord von Schlimmel," he said politely as he stood and bowed just a bit.

Without a greeting of his own, Lord von Schlimmel thrust a pair of boots into Gunther's hands. "I need these for a Christmas Eve ball."

Gunther opened his eyes wide. "But Christmas Eve is *tonight!*"

"Exactly!" said Lord von Schlimmel. "I shall need them by five o'clock."

Gunther turned the shoes over, his eyes taking in each detail. "But, Lord von Schlimmel, it's already one o'clock, and I see that there's a considerable amount—"

"I shall expect them to be done by *five o'clock!*" Lord von Schlimmel repeated imperiously. "Good day." And with that he swept grandly out the door in the same fashion in which he had entered.

Gunther stared after him, then down at the boots in his hand. He shook his head gloomily.

Gunther was still staring at the shoes when his cousin Griselda appeared at the door.

"What is this? My favorite cousin in the doldrums on Christmas Eve?" she exclaimed as she closed the door behind her. She stooped to place a large package on the floor inside.

Just then, from the opposite direction, the housekeeper appeared. The plump little woman cleared her throat. "Excuse me. I need to know about supper. Will there be anything special, it being Christmas Eve? Perhaps some stollen, and a few gingerbread—"

"Nein, nein!" Gunther sat down at his bench. "Soup is enough."

"If that's your wish then." With that she retreated as fast as her short legs would carry her. "Merry Christmas, Griselda," she called, disappearing toward the kitchen.

"And to you, Frau Dibble," Griselda responded warmly before turning back to see Gunther's grim expression.

"Gunther! It's Christmas Eve!" she scolded him, then continued sympathetically, "You miss your Hilda—and your little Karl, don't you."

Gunther slumped at his bench. *"Ja,* I do. But soon the holidays will be over." He tapped the boots before him. "Now I have these to repair for Lord von Hoity-Toity by five o'clock."

"Oh, dear Gunther!" Griselda moved toward him. "It's the day Jesus came to be with us." She put her hand on his arm. "Do you believe it?"

Gunther wrinkled his brow thoughtfully. "I suppose."

"Ach du lieber! I almost forgot!" Griselda ran to pick up the object she had brought. She whisked off its cover to reveal a gingerbread house. "Made by the children. Here!" She thrust it toward him. And with that she was gone.

Gunther stood in the middle of his shop, holding his gift. Griselda's good cheer made his own sadness seem greater. He looked down at the gift from the children. "Now what would I want with a gingerbread house?" he muttered.

Two hours later, Gunther was hard at work on Lord von Schlimmel's boots when Frau Dibble entered. "Mr. Gunther, you still want no lunch?"

"*Nein,*" he said without looking up, "my work isn't going well. These must be done by five o'clock."

"One would think we could have a little more cheer around here on Christmas Eve!" grumbled Frau Dibble as she left the room.

Gunther sighed deeply. He was very tired. Perhaps if he rested a few moments. . . . He put his head down on his arms.

Suddenly his shop door jingled. Gunther fought to drag himself from a sleepy stupor.

"Oh, my!" said a woman's voice. "He surely needs us!"

"He doesn't have a Christmas tree!" exclaimed a child.

"And there's nothing pretty in the window!" said another.

Raising his head, Gunther rubbed his hand across his eyes. "Good day."

"Merry Christmas!" responded the woman warmly.

"You've brought shoes?" he asked, rising from his bench.

"No shoes."

Gunther was puzzled. "Then you've come for something else?"

"Oh yes, definitely for something else," she said, removing her cloak. She took the children's wraps and laid them across a chair.

"This is Greta and Franz, and I'm Carrie," she said, smiling.

Gunther blinked as Carrie walked around inspecting things. "I'm Gunther, and . . ." He paused. "I've not seen you before. Where do you live?" he asked. He was slightly embarrassed to realize he was now following her about.

"Oh, somewhere on the edge of things, you might say." Carrie picked up a boot and peered at the window.

"I see," said Gunther, although he definitely did *not* see. The children seemed to be everywhere at once, and he had a feeling he might be losing control of his shop.

"Oh, look, Greta!" shrieked Franz, pointing.

"A gingerbread house!" cried Greta, running and kneeling before it.

Carrie spied a stool. "Ah, children, let's put it right up on this. There!" She cocked her head thoughtfully. "Gunther, don't you have a crèche—a manger scene?"

"It's—it's up in the attic."

"Why's it up there?" piped up Greta.

Gunther blinked. "Be—because Christmas doesn't seem happy anymore."

"Oh," said Greta.

Meanwhile, Carrie was again walking about the shop.

"Excuse me!" Gunther interjected, implying it was time for an explanation.

"Yes, of course," replied Carrie. "Don't worry; you're *not* in our way! Children!" she announced grandly, "run outside and bring the candle in!" She nodded at Gunther. "We wanted to look things over first."

"Of course!" Gunther let as much sarcasm creep into his voice as he dared. He sat down. Things were clearly out of his control.

Carrie smiled at him charmingly. "You'll like it very much. I know you will."

The children hurried back in, carrying a large, beautiful candle and a box.

Greta ran to Gunther. "Could I sit on your lap?"

"Well, *ja,* I suppose you may," he responded, surprised.

Greta settled herself. "Herr Gunther, did you ever have a little girl like me?"

"*Nein.* But I had a little boy. About the size of Franz."

"What was his name?"

"Karl," answered Gunther, not sure he wished to continue the conversation.

Greta nodded. "And did Karl have a mama?"

Franz snorted. "She asks so many questions!"

"It's all right, Franz," said Carrie, taking the candle from Greta. She knelt before the window, arranging greenery from the box around the candle. "It's good to talk about those things."

Gunther looked thoughtful. "Her name was Hilda."

"And did you love her very much?" asked Greta.

"Karl and I both did."

Franz came to stand beside Gunther. "I suppose they died, and that's what made Christmas not seem happy anymore."

"*Ja,*" Gunther replied softly.

Carrie gave the greenery a last pat and struck a match. The candle glowed with a wondrous light. "There now!"

Greta slid off Gunther's lap and ran to the window, shrieking, "It's beautiful!"

Gunther stood. It was time to get to the heart of things. "Excuse me! But would you mind telling me why you came here?"

"Because you needed us," Carrie replied simply.

"I see," he said, thinking that no, he did *not* see! "Then may I ask why you've put a candle in my window? My shop was perfectly fine without it!"

Carrie stepped back and surveyed the candle's glow for a long moment. "Well, it's like this. There's a beautiful old legend that the Christ Child walks about on Christmas Eve seeking to enter the hearts of men. And it's a candle in the window that invites Him across the threshold."

The children, on either side of Gunther, tugged at his arms. "Did you hear that story before, Herr Gunther?"

Gunther frowned.

"Oh, my!" cried Carrie. "It's time we were going. Come, children." She scooped up their wraps and started toward the door.

Franz stood his ground. "But, Carrie, you didn't tell him yet!"

Carrie stopped in her tracks. "Oh, mercy! You're so right. And it's the most important thing, too!" She walked back to Gunther, sat down, and waited for him to sit beside her. Then she put her hand on his arm and leaned toward him. "And this is what it is . . ."

Gunther swooshed about in a frenzy.

"Frau Dibble!" he boomed. "We need more evergreen boughs!"

His housekeeper appeared with an armload of greenery and a puzzled expression. "What's gotten into you?"

Gunther stopped abruptly. *"Ach du lieber!* We need stollen and cookies! Hurry! They must be done in time!"

"Stollen and cookies are already baking. I did them just in case." She started for the kitchen but stopped. "In time for what?"

"In time for my Visitor," Gunther replied.

"What visitor? You have people running in and out of here all the time."

Gunther smiled. "When my Visitor comes, you shall know it. I promise!"

"You've never seen this person?"

"Nein. But surely I will!"

Frau Dibble stared at the candle in the window. "That candle! I've never seen it before."

"Franz and Greta and Carrie brought it to me."

"Who are they?"

"I don't really know."

"Then where are they from?"

Gunther deposited the last evergreen bough beside the lantern. "They live somewhere on the edge of things."

Frau Dibble turned toward the kitchen and shook her head, muttering to herself.

"Go up to the attic and fetch the crèche," Gunther called after her.

"I already did. It's here in the hall," she said, bringing it to him.

Eagerly Gunther pulled back the flaps of the old dusty box. "What could be more appropriate for Him to see!"

The housekeeper cocked her head, listening intently. "Do you hear something outside? I'll go and look."

Frau Dibble soon reappeared with a frail woman. "I found her huddled outside."

In one bound Gunther was beside her. "Here, sit, please."

The woman sank down gratefully. "The candle in the window was so beautiful I had to stop and look. Then I felt faint."

Frau Dibble patted her shoulder comfortingly. "Sit here and rest."

The woman watched as Gunther went back to his unpacking. As he unwrapped the figure of an angel, the woman let out a cry of delight.

Gunther smiled. "Would you like to hold it?"

"Oh, could I?" She reached to stroke the wood. "When I was a child we lived next to a church that had figures like this."

A while later, afternoon had cast soft shadows into the shop. Gunther looked at the old woman, who still held the figurine in her hand.

His brow wrinkled in thought. "Would you like to take the crèche home with you?"

"Oh, I couldn't!"

"You could if I gave it to you."

The woman's lined face crinkled in wonderment. "A gift! For me? But why? It looks like you were putting it out for someone special."

Gunther was silent for a moment, then said softly, "I think He would want you to have it."

The old woman clasped the wooden figure to her, and tears coursed down her face. "It's the most wonderful gift I've ever had!"

Gunther smiled as he packed the crèche and sent the woman on her way. "Now, what else was it that I should be doing?" he said.

"Lord von Schlimmel's shoes?" Frau Dibble prompted.

Gunther cried out in horror. "In all the excitement, I forgot! I'll never be able to do them by five o'clock! Wait! What am I thinking? Lord von Schlimmel can dance in his stocking feet if need be!" Gunther strode about his shop. His face broke into a smile. "Why didn't I think of it before? I shall make a pair of shoes for the Christ Child! Is there enough time?"

Abruptly he clapped his hands. "The shoes for Prince Frederick!" The very finest pair he'd ever made! He need only make a few more stitches and finish off the lacings. The count would come for them next week. Surely he could make another pair for the little prince by then!

He retrieved the small shoes from a carved box on his shelf and went to work, breaking out in a joyful "Good Christian men rejoice . . ."

Some time later Gunther looked up to find a new visitor. The man's coat was threadbare, and he carried a large lumpy bag.

Gunther stood. "What may I do for you? Would you like to lay down your bundle?"

The man nodded, swinging it off his back. "Groceries for the family." He shifted uneasily. "Could I see some of your boots, perhaps?"

"*Ja, ja.*" Gunther picked up a pair of boots. "Now these are of the finest leather." Gunther stopped abruptly as he glanced again at the man's tattered clothing, then picked up another pair instead. "These may be patched and stitched up, but they are a fine pair of boots."

The man again shifted uncomfortably. "Well—I—let me think . . ."

"Actually, they've sat around here for so long, you would do me a great favor if you would take them for nothing." Gunther held them out. "Please!"

The man shook his head. "I have a confession to make. I have no money. I saw the candle in your window, and it looked so friendly that I came inside to get warm."

Gunther clapped him on the back. "Never mind that. You are welcome."

At that moment Frau Dibble entered.

"Frau Dibble, please get some milk and stollen for my guest."

She gaped in astonishment at the "guest." Then she pulled herself together and retreated to the kitchen.

"You're hungry, I think?" asked Gunther.

"*Ja*—I am." He glanced at his bag. "Those are not groceries."

"I thought as much."

The man sat down gratefully. "Those are scraps of wood I picked up for a fire in the stove. I shovel snow for money. Lately there has not been so much snow," he said with a grimace.

Frau Dibble appeared and placed a tray on the table.

"Eat," encouraged Gunther warmly. "Eat as much as you can!"

Shortly, there was a commotion outside of the shop. The door flew open and in swept Lord von Schlimmel. "I've come for my boots."

"And here they are." Gunther held his breath.

The man's eyes widened. "But, my dear fellow, you've scarcely done a thing to them!"

"Something more important came up."

Lord von Schlimmel glared at him. "But what do you expect me to do?"

Gunther put his arm around Lord von Schlimmel's shoulders, moving him jovially but firmly toward the door. "I expect you to dance in your stocking feet! Perhaps you will start a new style! And now—" Gunther opened the door. "Good night and Merry Christmas!" He closed the door on the confused nobleman.

When Gunther returned to the table, the beggar paused in his eating. "You're making shoes for someone more important than Lord von-Whoever?"

Gunther leaned across the table. "I'm waiting for the Christ Child. Do you think that I've taken leave of my senses?"

The beggar peered over his cup of milk. "You look quite sensible to me."

Gunther arose and took a worn Bible from the shelf. He tapped it lovingly. "In these pages, I find Him. And it comforts me here—in my heart."

"*Ja?* Even when things seem pretty bad?"

Gunther was thoughtful. "Sometimes I still feel very sad. But maybe not so much as if I didn't read. It helps."

The beggar munched slowly. "And now—you wait for Him? If you'll pardon my asking, why do you think He's coming here to you?"

"Someone came today to tell me so." Gunther glanced at the candle.

The beggar wiped his mouth with his hand and stood up. "I must go."

"Ah, then here are your boots. Please! You must take them! And I shall help you with your coat." Gunther looked down at the coat he held. How could he let anyone go out into the cold in such a coat? "Wait." He returned with a warm coat of his own. "Here, put this on."

"Oh, *nein!* How can I take your coat?"

"Take it! I have two coats. What would I want with two coats? One is plenty!"

The beggar buttoned it up in wonderment and picked up his bag. "You've given so much—the boots, a coat. You've given me food for my stomach and food for my soul. I'll not forget."

Gunther followed the man to the door. Large flakes fell silently. He could see no one. "Surely, He'll come soon," Gunther murmured. "In the meanwhile I must finish the shoes."

Soon a little girl entered. Gunther looked up. "You brought something for repair?"

When she shook her head, Gunther asked, "Well, what's your name?"

"Maria."

"Well, then, Maria, don't you think you should be going home?"

"I don't have a home."

Gunther tightened the last of his stitching. "Are you hungry?" he asked.

When Maria nodded solemnly he continued, "Do you see the cookies? And milk? You sit right down there and eat until you aren't hungry anymore."

The front door flew open, and in came Griselda. "Gunther, I'm back! Did you think I was never—" She stopped short. "Gunther! The greenery and—what on earth has happened? And I see you have a visitor!"

"That's Maria, who seems to have no home and who is very hungry."

Flinging off her cape and bonnet, Griselda sat down beside Maria. "Merry Christmas!" There was no response. "Why did you come in here?"

"Because I saw the pretty candle," Maria said, munching contentedly.

"The candle! Gunther, it's lovely! Where did it come from? And what caused you to put all these boughs about?"

Gunther started to polish the shoes. "It's a strange story. But it changed me—you see that?"

"I do see it!" she said with a smile.

He leaned forward. "I am expecting a visit from the dear Lord Himself! You think I'm crazy?"

Griselda surveyed him earnestly. "Never!" she said firmly.

"Oh!" With a cry of wonder, Maria ran to the gingerbread house.

Griselda knelt beside her. "It's a pretty little house, isn't it? What kind of house did you live in, Maria?"

"I lived in lots of houses."

"With your mama and papa?"

"*Nein.* I never saw them. With different people." The little girl gently touched the house. "The last lady said it cost too much to feed me."

A glance passed between Griselda and Gunther. Then Gunther laid the shoes down. His eyes caressed them proudly. "They are all done!"

Griselda stood up. "Then it's time for us to sing," she said. "Would you like that, Maria?"

When the last note died away, Maria said softly, "I liked your song."

"I must go now," said Griselda, tying on her bonnet. She moved to the little girl. "Maria, would you like to go home with me?"

For the first time Maria smiled. "*Ja,* I would like that."

"Then come." Griselda wrapped the tattered shawl around her. To Gunther she whispered, "I'll find out about her, Gunther, and who knows? Once one has six children, what's one more?" Griselda's face crinkled into a smile.

But Gunther was staring at Maria's feet. Slowly he walked to his cobbler's bench and picked up the shoes. He turned them over in his hands. "I think you need these, Maria. Perhaps you are the one I was supposed to make them for."

Maria sat down in wide-eyed astonishment as her rags were replaced by shoes. "I never had new shoes before! They're so beautiful!" She walked about, filled with happiness.

Griselda glanced at Gunther. "They were to be for the Christ Child?"

"He'll understand," Gunther replied. Now Maria was gazing at the gingerbread house. "Maria," he said, "would you like to take the gingerbread house with you? It could be your very own." He looked at Griselda.

"Oh, *ja,* your very own! What a lovely idea!"

When they had gone, Gunther walked about in the stillness of his shop. "The gingerbread house might have amused Him," he said aloud. "And surely He would have felt the crèche so special."

At his bench he picked up the carved shoe box and opened it. "And the shoes! The best pair I ever made!" Tears rolled down the cobbler's cheeks. "But He'll understand. I know He will!" He shut the empty box with a final snap and sat down.

Shadows were dark in the corners now. The candle glowed steadily, but the oil lamp sent fitful fingers of light over planks and beams. "*Ja,* Gunther," he said at last, "Christmas Eve will soon be over. And still He has not come."

Gunther had fallen asleep with his head on his arms when something woke him. He glanced toward the door, but all was quiet. He moved to the window and peered out. A blanket of snow lay tranquil and undisturbed around the shop.

He took out his pocket watch. "Just a few more minutes," he said sadly, "and I shall blow out the candle and go to bed."

He heard a sound behind him and whirled about, his heart leaping in hope.

Before him stood Carrie, Franz, and Greta. "Merry Christmas!" said Carrie.

He peered at them with a mixture of disbelief and puzzlement. "You've come back."

Carrie took her jacket off. "Of course!"

Gunther moved toward his cobbler's bench. "Please, do sit. Why have you returned?" he asked.

"To hear of your Christmas Eve, Gunther," Carrie responded.

"There's nothing to tell. No one came, but my cousin."

Carrie leaned forward. "No one else?"

"Not the Christ Child!" Gunther's frustration welled up inside him. He felt he would have cried if he were not a grown man. "Only a sick woman. And a street beggar. And a homeless child."

Carrie leaned back in her chair thoughtfully. "I see. Did you turn them away?"

Gunther stood up. "I couldn't turn them away! The beggar needed a coat, and I gave away the crèche and the shoes and—" He broke off and stared at Carrie in consternation. "Is that why He did not come? Because I gave away all the things that were to be His?"

Carrie jumped to her feet. "Oh, you mustn't think that!" She moved to the big Bible, which still lay on the table. "Look, Gunther. You must see this!"

Gunther looked at the passage in Matthew's Gospel and read aloud. "Then shall the King . . ." He looked questioningly at Carrie.

She nodded. "The dear Lord Jesus."

Gunther's finger followed as he read. "Then shall the King say 'Come, ye blessed, inherit the kingdom prepared for you. For I was hungry and ye fed me; I was thirsty, and ye gave me drink; I was a stranger, and ye took me in. Naked, and ye clothed me.'"

Gunther looked up, and his eyes brimmed with tears. "Those things are what I would have wanted to do for the Lord! If He had come, I would have done so!"

Carrie laid her hand on Gunther's shoulder. "I know you would have! But there's more." She nodded at Franz.

Franz got up solemnly. "Then shall the righteous say, 'Lord, when saw we thee hungered and fed thee or thirsty and gave thee drink? When saw we thee a stranger, and took thee in? Or naked, and clothed thee?'"

"And, Greta, how did the Lord answer?" prodded Carrie.

Greta moved until she was close and could look up into Gunther's face. "The King shall answer, 'Inasmuch as ye have done it unto one of the least of my brethren, ye have done it unto me.'"

Gunther stared from one to the other incredulously. "It says that?" he said.

Carrie pointed to the page. "It does! See here."

Gunther tried to adjust his mind to it all. "When I gave the shoes to Maria it was indeed for Him?"

Carrie nodded.

"And the coat—the crèche for the woman—the Christ Child came to me in these people?" He sat in hushed contemplation. "It makes one see things differently, doesn't it."

"It does!" Carrie moved toward the candle. "May I say an ancient candle prayer?" Gunther closed his eyes and listened.

"Lord Jesus, thou whose birth we celebrate, we have lit our candle in the presence of each other and the holy angels. Kindle in our hearts thy flame of love, that day shall break and shadows flee away. Amen."

When Gunther opened his eyes, Carrie and the children were gone. He stared about him. "In the presence of the holy angels?" he said aloud. Could it possibly be? Carrie and Franz and Greta?

Gunther stood up and walked to the candle and stared hard into the flame. Slowly he shook his head in wonder. "We have lit our candle, Lord Jesus, and you came!"

He knelt beside the window. "Kindle in my heart thy flame of love, that day shall break and shadows flee away," he murmered softly.

And Gunther looked into his heart and knew that it was so.